by
Elizabeth Levy
illustrated by
Mordicai Gerstein

Hyperion Books for Children
New York

Printed in the United States of America.

First Edition
1 3 5 7 9 10 8 6 4 2

Library of Congress Cataloging-in-Publication Data
    Something queer in the wild west / by Elizabeth Levy ; illustrated by
Mordicai Gerstein — 1st ed.
        p.   cm.
    Summary: While visiting her uncle's ranch in New Mexico, Gwen
follows her dog Fletcher at night to find out about the disappearance
of a thoroughbred horse.
    ISBN 0-7868-0258-8 (trade) — ISBN 0-7868-1117-X (pbk.)
    [1. Mystery and detective stories. 2. Horses—Fiction. 3. Dogs—
Fiction.] I. Gerstein, Mordicai, ill. II. Title.
PZ7.L5827Sk   1997   96-2554
[Fic]—dc20

The artwork for each picture is prepared using gouache and pen and ink.
This book is set in 13-point Bodoni Book.

Chapter One

Get Along, Little Doggies

"Get along, little doggies," sang Gwen and Jill as they rode their ponies on the range. Fletcher sat on top of a hay wagon. He howled along.

Gwen, Jill, and Fletcher were visiting Gwen's uncle Dale on a ranch in New Mexico. C. J., a boy who worked on the ranch, was teaching Gwen and Jill to ride.

C. J. turned to Fletcher. "Little doggies doesn't mean you, fella," he said, laughing. "Little doggies means little cows. Cowboys used to sing to the calves to keep them moving."

"Do you think Gwen and I can be cowgirls?" asked Jill.

"I don't see why not," said C. J.

By nightfall, Gwen and Jill discovered why cowgirls aren't made in a day. Gwen and Jill were a little sore—in fact, very sore. Fletcher was very tired, too. Riding on top of a hay wagon was exhausting. They all went to bed early.

CLOSE-UP OF GWEN'S WATCH →

"Cock-a-doodle-doo!" screeched a rooster in the middle of the night. "What's that?" groaned Jill. Gwen popped up in her bunk bed. She switched on the lighted dial of her watch. 3:31 A.M. Gwen tapped her braces. She

always tapped her braces when something queer was going on.

"I have a mystery to solve," Gwen announced at breakfast. "A rooster crowed in the middle of the night. In our books at school we learned that roosters crow at dawn."

C. J. laughed. And so did Gwen's uncle Dale.

"Gwen's very good at solving mysteries," argued Jill.

"Well, this isn't a mystery," said C. J. "Roosters crow whenever they feel like it. But I have a mystery for you—where's your dog?"

Gwen and Jill looked under the breakfast table. Fletcher wasn't there.

FLETCHER'S ABSENCE

They went outside to look for him. He wasn't in the barn by the house. Gwen and Jill saw some paw prints in the dust. "Fletcher! Fletcher!" Gwen and Jill shouted. The cows and ponies looked up. The mountain jays scolded in the cottonwoods. But there was no bark from Fletcher—not even a whimper.

Gwen and Jill followed the paw prints along a dried-up riverbed, called an arroyo.

FLETCHER'S
FOOT PRINTS

The paw prints ended at an old dilapidated barn on the far corner of the ranch. "Why is it all boarded up?" wondered Jill. "Do you think Fletcher's inside?"

Gwen tapped her braces.

Boom, boom, boom, rang out from inside the barn.

"What's making that sound?" wondered Gwen. Every time she tapped her braces there was an answering *Boom! Boom! Boom!*

"Fletcher!" shouted Jill. She was getting worried.

"Look!" exclaimed Jill. She pointed to a hole by the bottom of the barn door. A black nose appeared. Fletcher squirmed out from under the wall of the barn. Little bits of hay stuck to his fur. Jill flung her arms around him.

"Fletcher, what were you doing in that old barn?" asked Jill. Fletcher wagged his tail.

"Something queer is in that barn," said Gwen. "Let's see what it is!"

(TAIL WAGGING) ↓

10

Before they could figure out a way to get inside, C. J. cantered up on his horse. "What are you doing here?" he asked. He sounded worried. "Come on, I'll give you all a ride back."

"Something's inside that old barn making lots of noise," protested Gwen. "We want to explore."

"It's probably just bats," said C. J.

Jill put her hands to her hair. "Not bats!" screeched Jill. "I'm scared of bats."

"Then we'd better get away from here," said C. J. quickly. He scooped up Gwen and Jill and told them to hang on. "Come on, little doggie," C. J. called to Fletcher. Fletcher trotted along, stopping every once in a while to smell the wildflowers.

Chapter Two

The Legend of the Wild Horse

C. J. stopped to let his horse take a drink from a mountain stream.

"You really shouldn't be afraid of bats, Jill," said Gwen. "I read in school that bats don't dive-bomb for your hair. They have radar so that they won't bump into things. We should go back to that barn. It looked really old."

"It is more than five hundred years old," said C. J. "The Spanish conquistadores built that barn when they came up from Mexico. But I wouldn't go back there. In fact, you shouldn't even go near there." C. J. paused. "That barn's haunted," he added.

"First bats. Now haunted!" whispered Jill in an awed voice.

Gwen looked at C. J. suspiciously. She began to tap her braces.

"I don't believe the barn's haunted," said Gwen. "We're not little kids. We weren't born yesterday."

"That barn really *is* haunted," said C. J. "It's haunted by the ghost of wild horses. Hundreds of years ago, the wildest horse of them all was a prisoner in that barn. She was so wild, nobody could ride her. Her master was a Spaniard. He was sure he could break her spirit. He kept her in that barn and tried to break her. But he couldn't. The horse kicked the door in, and it fell on her master."

"What happened to the mare?" asked Gwen.

"She broke free. There is still a herd of wild horses in the canyon who are descended from her," said C. J. "The wildest horses of all come from that one wild mare. They are so powerful and beautiful that if you see one, you'll never be the same."

That night, Gwen asked her uncle if it was true. "Is that boarded-up barn haunted by the ghost of a wild horse?"

"That's the legend," said Uncle Dale. "That barn is supposed to be bad luck to anyone who tries to keep a horse in it. It might be true. My boss, Mr. Moses, used to keep his show horses in that barn. Just a couple of months ago one of his horses nearly killed him. He moved his show horses closer to town. The barn's empty now.

"Are some horses so wild that if you see one you'll never be the same?" asked Jill.

"I've heard that legend, too," said Uncle Dale. "But I've never seen a horse that wild. There are supposed to be some wild horses up in one of the canyons, but I've never seen them."

15

That night, Jill shook Gwen awake. "Is it the silly rooster again?" asked Gwen, still half asleep.

"No," said Jill. "It's Fletcher. He was sleeping at the foot of my bed, and now he's gone."

"Do you think he went back to that old barn?" asked Gwen.

Gwen and Jill pressed their noses against the window. By the light of the full moon, they saw a horse galloping on the hillside. Its white mane and tail were flying. In the distance they heard mournful howling. It sounded like a coyote, but different—a little lower pitched and a slightly flatter sound.

Chapter Three

Guilty?!

At dawn, Fletcher came home. His paws were dusty. He lay on the kitchen floor twitching and making grunting noises as if he was having weird dreams.

"I wonder what he's dreaming about?" asked Gwen, tapping her braces.

"Animals are like people," said C. J. "They dream about what makes them happy and sad."

"Fletcher must be dreaming about salami," joked Uncle Dale.

"I don't think so," said Jill. "I think he's dreaming about the horse we saw."

"A horse made of salami?" cracked Uncle Dale.

"It was all white," said Gwen.

"I don't have any white horses," said Uncle Dale.

The next night, Fletcher disappeared again. When he came back at dawn, he looked even more tired than before.

Jill patted his panting side. "This isn't like him," said Jill. "At home, he sleeps on my bed all night."

"And most of the day," Gwen added.

"I wouldn't worry about him," said Uncle Dale. "He's just roaming the range."

Gwen and Jill looked at each other.

"Fletcher doesn't roam," said Gwen. She tapped her braces and looked at Fletcher suspiciously.

Gwen read the local weekly newspaper. "Listen to this," she said. "'A hundred-thousand-dollar show horse named Espíritu reported stolen by Steven Moses.'"

"Steven Moses is the man who owns this ranch," said Uncle Dale. "Espíritu is his champion horse."

"What color is Espíritu?" asked Gwen.

"White," said Uncle Dale. .

Gwen began to tap her braces.

"Do you think Espíritu could be the horse we saw at night in the moonlight?" asked Jill.

Gwen and Jill looked at Fletcher. He was dreaming, and his little legs were moving faster and faster.

"Would you two like to take a riding lesson this morning?" asked C. J. "You were doing really well."

"Sure," said Gwen and Jill. They helped C. J. saddle and bridle their ponies. C. J. taught the girls how to

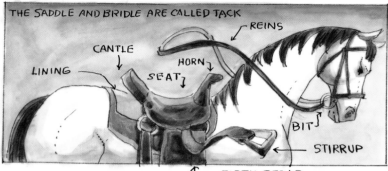

THE SADDLE AND BRIDLE ARE CALLED TACK

REINS

CANTLE

HORN

LINING

SEAT

BIT

STIRRUP

GIRTH STRAP

DOING FIGURE EIGHTS

neck-rein. He had them practice figure eights around barrels just the way the cowgirls did in the rodeo. It was so much fun that Gwen and Jill almost forgot about the white horse. Fletcher slept in the shade.

Just as they were about to finish, a black-and-white car with the word SHERIFF on the door turned into the driveway, kicking up dust around its tires. The car screeched to a halt. The sheriff got out, followed by a man with a deep tan, wearing English-style riding clothes. The sheriff waved C. J. over. The sheriff looked calm, but the other man looked angry.

"I wonder why the sheriff wants to talk to C. J.?" asked Gwen. She started to tap her braces, but her pony shook his head at the sound of Gwen's tapping.

"Whoa!" said Gwen, grabbing the horn of her saddle to hold on.

TAP
TAP
TAP
TAP
TAP
TAP

The sheriff and the man went into the ranch house to talk to Uncle Dale. C. J. came back to help Gwen and Jill off their ponies. "What was that guy so mad about?" Gwen asked. "He looked as mad as a hornet."

"I'd like to see him stung by a hornet," muttered C. J. "He wins lots of blue ribbons, but he doesn't really know horses. I once saw him tie a rope around a horse's neck and beat him because the horse threw him."

Uncle Dale came out of the ranch house, followed by the sheriff and Mr. Moses.

"Gwen and Jill?" shouted Uncle Dale. "The sheriff wants to ask you some questions."

Fletcher rolled over and opened one eye. He followed Gwen and Jill over to talk to the sheriff. Gwen realized that C. J. had never really told her what the sheriff had wanted.

"We haven't done anything wrong, have we?" Jill
whispered to Gwen.

"Not that I know of," Gwen whispered back.

"Then why do I feel guilty?" asked Jill.

"I have this creepy buzzing sound in my ear," said
Gwen. "It seems to be telling me to be careful."

"Your uncle says that the two of you saw a white stallion around here. Is that true?" asked the sheriff sternly.

Gwen and Jill looked at each other.

24

"It was just a dream," said Gwen. Jill nodded.

Fletcher twitched his ears. He looked worried.

The sheriff scratched his head. Fletcher scratched behind his ear. Mr. Moses made a face. Fletcher yawned.

Mr. Moses looked at Gwen's uncle. "You said these girls talked about a white stallion. Espíritu is a pure white Thoroughbred worth thousands of dollars. . . . What's going on here?"

"Girls dream about horses all the time," said Uncle Dale. "Just the way animals dream."

"Well, if these girls keep dreaming about a white stallion, I want to know about it."

Gwen swatted at her ears. The buzzing sound was louder. Fletcher swatted his ear with his paw. He crawled closer to Gwen and Jill.

NOTE: HORNETS ARE A KIND OF WASP WITH A VERY STRONG STING.

Suddenly Mr. Moses started to wave his hands in the air frantically. "Hornets!" he screamed. "I'm allergic to hornets."

"Then you'd better leave," said Uncle Dale. "The ranch is full of hornets this summer."

Uncle Dale walked Mr. Moses over to the sheriff's car. "I'll be back," said Mr. Moses. "I want to look over the property—maybe Espíritu escaped and broke his darned neck. I'd almost rather he was dead."

"Sure," said Uncle Dale. "Then you could sting the insurance company."

"What?" demanded Mr. Moses.

"You'd better get going. I want to be sure you don't get stung," said Uncle Dale.

HORNETS →

"Uncle Dale, why would Mr. Moses want a dead horse?" Gwen asked.

"If the horse is dead, he can collect the insurance money," said Uncle Dale. "I hope Espíritu is far gone from here." Uncle Dale went into the house.

Gwen started to tap her braces. Jill stared at her. "You don't really think the stallion we saw was a dream, do you?" asked Jill.

Gwen looked down at Fletcher. "Tonight we're going to stay up all night and see where he goes."

Fletcher rolled over on his back. He certainly didn't look like a dog who would go anywhere.

Chapter Four
Rats and Bats

That night, Gwen and Jill went to their room, but they didn't get ready for bed. Fletcher lay down on Jill's bunk.

Gwen and Jill didn't go to bed at all. They sat on the hard floor and read scary stories out loud to each other. Fletcher curled into a ball and fell sound asleep.

"Maybe he's not going anywhere tonight," said Jill with a yawn. She looked at her watch. It was almost midnight. She was very tired. Even the scary stories couldn't keep her awake. Gwen was tired, too.

They couldn't help it. They crawled into their bunks and closed their eyes.

Soon Jill felt four paws plunk on her stomach. She opened her eyes and poked Gwen's bunk with a broom handle. Fletcher was on the move. He hopped out the window. They followed him as he walked along the dried-up arroyo. They were going toward the old barn that C. J. had told them was haunted.

They heard a loud whinny. Fletcher's tail began wagging very quickly. He did something Gwen and Jill had rarely seen him do. He started to trot. He trotted right up the embankment.

Gwen and Jill peered through the tall grass. They heard hooves pounding closer. Someone was riding a white stallion bareback. The rider reached down and picked up something with a long nose and a fat belly.

Fletcher! Fletcher sat on the stallion in front of the rider. They galloped into a canyon. Gwen and Jill stared at each other. Gwen tapped her braces. The braces felt cold and real. This was not a dream.

The next morning Uncle Dale asked Gwen and Jill if they wanted to come to town with him. "No," said Gwen quickly. "We'll stick around here."

As soon as Uncle Dale left, Gwen said, "We've got to find that horse we saw Fletcher riding. And we've got to find out who was riding him bareback. I think the secret is in the old barn. Let's go see what's inside."

"The barn's supposed to be haunted," said Jill. "Maybe Fletcher is under a spell. Maybe he saw one of those horses that you're not supposed to see," she added.

"The horse we saw was *not* a ghost," said Gwen.

Gwen and Jill took off toward the haunted barn.

They pushed on the door. It wouldn't budge. "Look," said Gwen, tapping her braces. She pointed to a lock. "It's a combination lock. I don't think they had shiny combination locks in the fifteenth century. Somebody's keeping something in there—and they don't want us to see what it is."

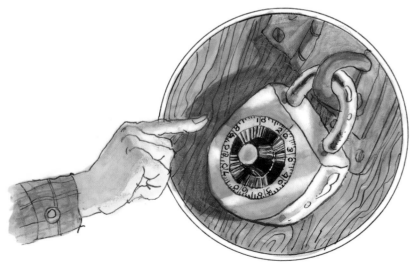

"Maybe we can go in the way Fletcher did," said Jill.

"Great idea!" said Gwen. Gwen got down on her tummy and slithered through the hole under the foundation. Jill followed her. "Uh-oh," whispered Gwen from the other side.

Jill stopped halfway through the hole. "What do you mean, 'Uh–oh'? Bats?"

"Bats are the least of it," said Gwen. "This is a big uh-oh."

Jill slithered through to the other side and stood next to Gwen. In the dusky light of the centuries-old barn, bats were flitting about in the high beams. But Gwen was right. The bats were the least of it. A huge white stallion was stomping its front hooves. Its nostrils flared angrily.

"Nice horsey," whispered Gwen.

"I don't think he's so nice," said Jill in a scared voice.

The stallion snorted again. "Something queer is going on," said Gwen. "And it has something to do with this wild horse."

"Yeah, and we may never be the same," said Jill. "We may be dead."

FLETCHER
BETWEEN THE STALLION'S
HOOVES

Gwen and Jill heard something rustle in the hay.

"Just what we need now—rats!" hissed Jill. "Rats and bats!"

A black nose came out from under the hay. Fletcher stretched. His big belly nearly scraped the floor of the barn. He walked right between the stallion's legs.

"Fletcher, you'll get killed!" cried Jill.

Chapter Five

Home on the Range

The stallion stopped snorting. It bent its magnificent neck, and its lips seemed to kiss the top of Fletcher's head.

"He likes Fletcher," whispered Gwen.

"Love is more like it," said a voice behind them.

Gwen and Jill twirled around. It was C. J. He patted the stallion's neck. "I couldn't go near Espíritu until Fletcher came along," he said.

Gwen tapped her braces. "Espíritu is the name of the horse that Mr. Moses is looking for," said Gwen. "You've been hiding him here, and you tried to keep us away by telling us the barn was haunted."

"*Espíritu* means
'spirit' in Spanish. Mr.
Moses tried to break
Espíritu's spirit. I couldn't
stand the way Mr. Moses
mistreated him," admitted
C. J. "I've been letting
him hide here until I can
set him free."

"So that's why you
told us the barn was
haunted," said Gwen, tap-
ping her braces.

Espíritu kicked out at
the bucket by his hooves.
"That's the *'boom, boom,
boom'* we heard the first
day," said Gwen.

"I didn't lie to you
about this barn being
haunted," said C. J. "It's a
true story about the wild
mare. My grandfather told
it to me. The day after you
all got here, I found
Fletcher sleeping under
Espíritu's legs." It happens
like that sometimes—

high-strung animals like Espíritu calm down with a dog or a cat. Espíritu doesn't like to go anywhere without Fletcher."

"If you couldn't go near Espíritu until Fletcher got there, how did Espíritu get into the barn?" asked Gwen.

"He came back to this barn on his own," said C. J., looking around. "I think he knew he'd be safe here. Maybe he knew that the legend of the wild horse would protect him."

Gwen asked, "What are you going to do with Espíritu?"

"I've been getting Espíritu used to the range," explained C. J. "Fletcher comes with us. I've got to let Espíritu go tonight. It's too dangerous to keep him. Mr. Moses suspects something. I need your help . . . or at least Fletcher's. The only way that Espíritu will go quietly is if Fletcher goes with him."

"We'll help," said Gwen and Jill together. "Fletcher would want us to. I think he likes Espíritu."

"I think they love each other," said C. J.

Gwen and Jill looked a little jealous.

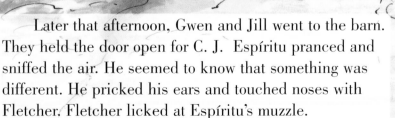

Later that afternoon, Gwen and Jill went to the barn. They held the door open for C. J. Espíritu pranced and sniffed the air. He seemed to know that something was different. He pricked his ears and touched noses with Fletcher. Fletcher licked at Espíritu's muzzle.

"Someone's coming!" said Jill, pointing down the hill.

On the dusty road, they could see a Jeep. "Quick!" said C. J. "We've got to get Espíritu out of here."

C. J. hopped onto Espíritu's back. "Come on," he said to Gwen and Jill, leaning down for them. "I don't want you two to get in trouble."

Gwen and Jill hopped on behind C. J. With Fletcher next to him, Espíritu took off. "Look at Fletcher!" exclaimed Jill. Fletcher was running through the brush—his legs stretched out to their fullest.

"He wants Espíritu to be free!" cried Gwen into the wind.

The Jeep followed. Through gullies and arroyos, the Jeep bumped and jolted. Fletcher led them into a narrow canyon—so narrow the Jeep couldn't get through.

Espíritu stopped and C. J. slipped the halter off his head. Gwen and Jill slid off his back. Espíritu bent his

noble neck and nuzzled Fletcher. Then he whinnied. In the distance a horse whinnied back. "That's the band of wild horses. Espíritu will join them," whispered C. J.

After they watched Espíritu trot off, C. J. told Gwen and Jill to follow him. He led them back to the ranch along a narrow footpath, circling high above the Jeep. A few minutes after they got back to the ranch house, an angry Mr. Moses jammed on the brakes of his Jeep and leaned on his horn. Uncle Dale came out on the porch and invited Mr. Moses inside the house.

"I saw Espíritu!" yelled Mr. Moses. "I came back to check if anybody had spotted him, and your girls were riding him. That dog and those girls and that boy—they were all roaming out on the range."

Uncle Dale looked down at Fletcher, who had fallen asleep, exhausted. His legs were twitching. "This dog roams the range only in his dreams," said Uncle Dale.

"But . . . but," sputtered Mr. Moses.

"But nothing," said Uncle Dale, swatting at the air. "Looks like the hornets are out something fierce. Guess you'd better go file your insurance claim."

"I saw that dog running toward Wild Horse Canyon— leading Espíritu!"

Fletcher rolled over with his legs in the air.

Uncle Dale scratched Fletcher's belly. "This dog sure loves his sleep."

Mr. Moses stared at Fletcher.

"Look at him," said Uncle Dale to Mr. Moses. "Fletcher is *not* a running hound."

"I guess you're right," admitted Mr. Moses.

"Thanks, Uncle Dale," said Gwen after Mr. Moses left.

"That man didn't deserve a horse like Espíritu," said Uncle Dale. "He'll probably be able to collect the insurance money eventually—and that's more than a man like that deserves. Now let's get ready for dinner. Tonight should be an early night. I don't want to send you girls back home all tuckered out. After all, I want you to come back next year."

Just at dawn Gwen woke Jill up. "What?" asked Jill. "Not another rooster. Or has Fletcher gone missing again?"

"No," whispered Gwen. "But look at him. Fletcher does love something more than sleep."

Fletcher had his front paws on the windowsill. He

lifted his head and howled. In the distance they all heard a whinny. Gwen and Jill looked out the window. High on a hill, they saw a silhouette of a wild stallion.

Espíritu was free—at home on the range.

Gwen and Jill looked down at Fletcher. He wagged his tail. He seemed to be trying to tell them that he had enough love inside of him for everybody.